Lockdown

Innit

Poems about
Absurdity

M J Mallon

Published in Paperback March 2021 — ISBN:978-1-9998224-0-8

Published in Kindle February 2021

Kyrosmagica Publishing

mjmallon.com

DEDICATION

This dedication is for us all, wherever we live in the world. To my family for making my lockdown more agreeable. To my eldest daughter for encouraging us to exercise, jog and take part in yoga! To my youngest daughter for beautifying us by painting our lockdown nails and to my hubby for playing the best music to keep us entertained.

I hope this collection will bring you some cheer and food for thought, when we need it the most. Within these pages you will find poems on the absurdity and frustration experienced during our lockdown lives, some of which I hope will make you laugh. Hopefully, there is something for everyone. Stay safe and well. x

PRAISE FOR

LOCKDOWN INNIT

Lockdown innit is a wonderful collection of predominantly free verse poetry on all kinds of themes experienced during the author's third lockdown. I am sure many of the pieces will resonate with readers who have also experienced humanities frustrating behaviours during this pandemic.

The discarded masks rolling down the roads and the impact of this on wildlife in the future when landfills are filled, and oceans invariably get full of them is certainly something that has crossed my mind. (Simply cutting off the side strings from the masks before throwing disposable ones away could make a big difference so they don't get tangled on wildlife!) I've also had my fair share of dealing with drivers filled with road rage, presumably from the stress!

The varied mood and tone of the pieces is equally matched with the lovely presentation and wonderful splashes of humour. Emotive and descriptive language is employed to engage our senses and of course my favourite piece is probably 'This Face.' Making this a highly enjoyable collection and one I have no doubt in recommending! **Author Sarah Northwood**

An intricate mix of observations from the author about how the pandemic has brought change. Some welcome, some not so much. A thought provoking read. A short book and quick read. The content is about the author's thoughts on lockdown and how it affected her and others around her. Well written poetry and a book I'd recommend to others. **Author Lizzie Chantree**

I loved the poems, they captured the spirit of the times, the vagaries of human behaviour, the poignant signs of a society in change. There are some beautiful observations of what has become the new normal. **Author Richard Dee**

TABLE OF CONTENTS

PREFACE

Lockdown Innit is a collection of poems set during my third period of captivity in the UK. With three stints with little or no freedom, it is no wonder that Lockdown Innit came to mind.

During the first lockdown in the UK I compiled my first anthology, This Is Lockdown, to include my personal diaries, poetry, and flash fiction plus contributions from 28 authors, bloggers and creatives. It was a great way to engage with other writers during this time and to discover new authors to read! This is Lockdown is available in kindle and a shorter version in paperback.

I hope this short collection of poetry might make you laugh, ponder and smile. And I hope I don't upset any joggers. I love you really. How could I not? My daughter's one!

LOCKDOWN BREEZE

"Lockdown innit!" Rita remarked pegging washing out,
Graham groaned, smothering a sob,
The wind puffed a mighty grunt,
Which billowed under Rita's skirts as they sailed up.
The wind blew and blew,
As the clothes line danced,
The pegs grinned, opening wide, releasing,
Sheets, bras, assorted lingerie and pants.

The wind held its breath but couldn't resist,
Gasping, it let out one last guffaw,
A racy suspender belt landed on Rita's head,
And lacy, skimpy knickers tickled Graham's stubbly chin,
Neighbours Alex and Andria,peered above the fence,
Gasping, jaws dropping. "My lingerie," Andria said,
The wind's cheeks puffed out. He'd done an almighty job,
Each time the wind blows they'll remember him.
And his unforgettable lockdown breeze!

A HUG FROM ME TO YOU

We cried and cried the day you left
I wish I could keep you with me
I call and call to say hello
But more than that
I keep this hug
Here for
You.

It
Is safe
To say love
How very much you
Mean to me, so come back soon
Bring that hug with you for me to share
These open arms await your sunny smile.

To my daughter, Gina, missing you. x

SUPERMARKET BOZOS

The supermarket bozos come in pairs,
Or sometimes two times two makes four,
No mask, no commonsense,
No gloves, at all.
Nana Nora scowls. She ain't afraid of them,
Nor of the germs they carry.

"Security!Take your fag break. Now! I'll Mask them up.
And karate chop those bozos bones, you'll see!"
The Bozos may be tough but they're wicked feared,
They shy away, saying, "Nana Nora's
Wicked tongue ain't shy."
"Eighty four, her boot kick's mighty scary high!"

For my mum who has witnessed her fair share of bozos. x

THE FACE MASK ROLLS

It rolls, the face mask.

Picking up speed and dust on the road,

Discarded,

Thrown out the driver's car window.

The owner, a non smoker, has no fag to throw.

It stops, flattened by cars, alone it sits.

Intact, no ears to caress, or lipstick to smear.

Forgotten sweat lurks under its blue surface.

Microscopic dead skin cells mowed down by wheels,

Elasticity defunct, no snotty nose to cover.

The sun glows,

Despairing,

It burns.

Until in feigned forgiveness it accepts,

Human transgressions. The sun sighs,the rain spits.

In a garden, a black face mask,

Newly bought,

Dropped perhaps?

Tossed beside the flower bed.

Looks expensive.

Not disposable. Reusable.

I wonder, what it's doing there.

Was it part of a conspiratorial pair?

Or did its owner prefer a single,

To be reused again and again,

Filthy selfish bugger.

The sun winks.

As clouds part,

Threatening a downpour.

In the supermarket car park,

Witness a new kind of rock and roll,

Face masks and gloves,

Doing a manic Saturday Fever dance,

As cars slide into place.

Shoppers push trolleys past.

Remembered queues gone.

Just one person ahead perhaps.

Squirting sanitiser and disinfectant,

All good. Their nice, fresh, clean, trolley,

Unlike his, loaded to the brim with selfish ignorance.

No room for food.

The sun departs,

Only shadows,

And the threat of death remains.

As the unmasked user pushes his trolley,

He coughs, rubs his nose and moves on.

ROAD RAGE DURING COVID19

The range rover is shiny and bright,

Showing off, gleaming,

The driver not so, he scowls.

Judging us first. I judge him too. I'll never trade you.

My old people carrier. LOVEABLE.

Scratches, rust and mishaps,

Font of memories: kids outings, long distance escapades.

Life when we were young. And smiling.

Parties, sleepovers, concerts, and drama,

Sleep deprivation.

Lifts in mum's taxi to who knows where,

When and Why? Sweet, forgotten times. Good times.

And now. COVID19. This. Crap. Give. Me. Strength.

The range rover,

Purposely obscures our view.

Driven by a person. I can't.

I don't want to see. Who you are is so apparent.

You. Git. I clench my teeth.

We wait for a safe gap,

On our way,

To a special night out.

Just us, no kids. We're empty-nesters on the razzle dazzle.

I stare at my painted nails and high heels.

But now, we aren't so sure.

Threatened. I tremble, fearing a road rage battle.

My husband honks his horn.

The plonker revs his engine.

Off he goes,

Trailing a blast of fury.

One step further in his journey to God knows where.

Idiot. Who is in that car with you? Are they safe?

And for what? Spoil my dinner?

No, you won't.

Selfish doesn't win. Bullies don't either.

Even when they seem to.

My car and I move on, ready to forget you.

Poor them. Poor us. Selfish.

I hope you don't kill anyone.

Sometimes the virus has friends to do its job.

⸺

This is based on a true event at a time between lockdowns when we were able to go out to a restaurant.

DANGER TO PEDESTRIANS

This jogging lark makes me mad,
Innocent pedestrians. Our eyes ahead,
We couldn't see you from behind.
Your "For Fucks Sake," took us by surprise!
What did we do to aggrieve you so?

We moved by to give you space,
A minor delay in making way,
Surely, we deserve to be forgiven?
Instead, you spew spit as you jog past.
Spoiling this, our peaceful day.

I swear if by chance we happen upon you again,
I may just kick your butt,
Trip you up. Block your way, yell,
Urge you to ring a bell,
Or, blow a loud, I'm here, idiot whistle!

Unfortunately, this happened to my daughter and I when we were taking a walk. A jogger swore, and then spat just a few feet away from us.

JOGGING APP

If jogging with my daughter,
Leaves my knees in mind to stay at home
My back agrees to follow suit
And so does my poor heart too…
A disembodied voice cries, "Don't give up!"
So I continue , as best I can,
Jogging dearest, panting,
Trying to catch up with you!

We use a friendly app,
The lady has a cheery voice,
Offers snack rewards to finish,
Sounds so easy, to walk then run,
I'm tempted to switch her off!
But no chance, you'd know.
My personal trainer, dear daughter.
Shouldn't be — never should be you!

For my daughter, Natasha. Hope it makes you smile. x

A LITTLE LIBRARY

Where would we be without you?
Little library,
Four dear shelves,
Stacked with mysterious worlds.

What shall I read today?
And where will you take me....
A romance perhaps,
Or a horror, could be a fantasy,
Shall we have murder, magic, delight?

A cabinet of mysteries, a paranormal,
Out of reach, a crime?
Could you be a memoir,
Or a learned tome? A hidden diary?
Whatever you might be,
I will come back again,
Little Library,
And reach deep within your shelves,
For a bounty of hidden, wondrous tales.

BREAST LUMP

In a shower I found you,
A lump in my breast, a large one.
My heart groaned in fear, holding back a tear,
I rang my GP, got a different doctor.
Sounded covid stressed but invited me in,
Which I did, without delay,
Prodding and poking, asking me questions.

His expression serious and somewhat uncertain,
He announced off to hospital as soon as,
A scan, a mammogram.
So I did as he said, of course.
There, I sat in the wrong seat along a long hallway,
Socially distanced apart, masks on.
Ladies, of varying ages, some so young.
Waiting for news. Poor dears.

The mammographer seemed confused,
How come you didn't notice this?
Where you really so busy?
My heart sank as I realised my dire folly,
Back to the waiting. Tick Tock, I prepared myself,
Expecting the worst, my eyes sneaked a peek at,
Ladies like me, all scared, all uncertain.

They drew some fluid,
And some more, and some more.
Kept on adding more vials. How absurd.
Until there was no liquid left.
With a smile they said,
It's benign, just a huge cyst,

I smiled, with such utter relief.

Left that clinic on air, light,
My fear diminishing but….
A guilty voice clamoured,
Hear me, it said, there are others still there,
With their consoling cups of tea,
Coming to terms with dreadful news,
News we never, ever want to hear.

To everyone waiting for news, and to those with a cancer diagnosis. This time is hard enough. To my dear friends who are currently fighting their battle with cancer. Sending love that you will beat cancer's butt.x

MONDAY BLUES

I forgot today is Monday,
Thought it was a rest day,
Left my cares on sleep mode,
And snoozed until I might awake,
To catch and tag the next day.

Work forgot to miss me,
Emails, zooming in the background,
So my conscience logged me on,
Praying I'd find my long lost team,
Who might remember me!

Writing in a daily diary,
Helps reminds me which day's which,
With its stickers, and pretty shapes,
It makes me sing like this,
Turn the page to.... Monday.

Monday's never a fun day,
Tuesday's better than a Monday,
Wednesday's half way, each way,
Thursday's getting in the groove day,
Friday's piss off yell, off licence, play.

Saturday's boozy, sore head, staggers ahead,
Sunday's nearly Monday, so off you go,
And then to and fro, are we ready?
For Monday , here it comes again,
Waiting for tomorrow's Tuesday to wake us up!

THE AUTHOR ZOOM

No one else gets us,
So we writers zoom together,
Chatting about books,
Plots, characters, arcs, sub-plots,
Marketing trials and reviews!

Sometimes we read too,
Short passages from our work,
Five minutes, only,
Don't make it too long lovely,
I have dinner to prepare!

I've had the pleasure of taking part in two zoom groups: Charli Mills Carrot Ranch 5 at the Mic, and Tracie's Barton-Barrett's International author zoom group. I am also intending to start a zoom group too.

SWAN'S CONFUSION

(TANKA)

Did you see that swan?
Beauty, posing by a bin,
White against the green.
Hurry up, come over, quick.
He's guarding that green waste bin!

How could that happen?
A swan escapes the river?
It's lockdown innit,
Anything is possible,
And nothing's at all certain!

HORSES LIKE STATUES
(BUTTERFLY CINQUAIN)

.

Horses
Grazing on grass
Unaware they are watched
Still, like symmetrical statues
Nose down
Three leafy shrubs oddly aligned
How bizarre this scene is
My eyes observe
Lockdown

PRAYING FOR A MIRACLE (DAISY CHAIN POEM)

Miracles? There will be no miracles here,
Here our simple wish is for a hot drink and a scone,
Scone, Brownie, Cake, "Sorry! Impossible, the gallery's closed."
Closed to the thirsty, hungry public, only a portable van,
Van with an open hatch, doors wide, allows access to hot drinks."
Drinks, warm us as we sit together outside in the cold.
Cold wind nips as we revisit memories of past visits, laughter,
Laughter! In the distance, we see a tiny figure,
"Miracles," he yells defiantly, there will be miracles !

This poem is inspired by Nathan Coley's installation:
There will be no miracles here which is situated at the Scottish
Gallery of modern Art (Modern Two,) in Edinburgh. After the
first lockdown we were disappointed to find it was still closed.
We've spent many happy days at these art galleries in Edinburgh.

BUCKET LIST

Our bucket list is short but swell,
We colour code ideas one by one,
Beginning each new day, or evening with,
Ticks for... Prize activities!
Spa Day and Rom Com,
Netflix and chill,
Cocktails and Karaoke,
Scary movie night and let's make pizza,
Binge watch Friday Night Dinner,
Bake brownies and biscuits,
Board games,
Group Yoga,
Pancakes and French Toast Brunch,
We rotate and change them all,
But the best we cherish,
We repeat Funday Sunday Brunch!

This idea came to me via my eldest daughter, who mentioned that her student flat mates had created a beautifully colour coded bucket list

VIOLIN PLAYER ON A TIGHTROPE

DECASTICH—EGG TIMER POEM

Man without a mask
On a tightrope
Violin
Playing
Song
Song
Playing
Violin
On a Tightrope
Man without a mask

THIS FACE

Here's my face, I'm in the pink,
A shade lighter here and there,
Black glasses, hint of eyebrows,
Smile of lipstick, small detail of nose,
Black border for my chin and hair.
Sweet perfection, not a hair out of place!

Sweet perfection, without any disgrace!
Could that really be me in there?
I didn't even brush my hair!
Or wipe the gunk off my specs,
Those eyebrows, freshly tweeked,
My hair bobbed, cut to perfection.
Which angel darling created this?

Thank you to author and poet Sarah Northwood
for creating this image for me. x

THIS AUTHOR
LONGS FOR PETS
ETHEREE POEM

Pets!
See that,
Ginger cat,
Cute fluffed curled ball,
Welcome visitor,
On a bench he's dreaming,
Adventuring faraway,
If only I could sneek a peek!
Oh, if only I could travel far!
Please magic me away into your dreams.

REVIEWS

I hope that you enjoyed this collection of poetry. It is part of a series of books I've written during Lockdown. The first being an anthology of diaries, short stories and poetry: *This Is Lockdown* which released in kindle July 2020. The anthology, *This Is Lockdown* The anthology, *This Is Lockdown* features many international authors, bloggers and creatives. It is now also available in a shorter version in paperback.

I'd love it if you would leave a review of *Lockdown Innit* on the relevant sites. Reviews are like gold dust to authors.

Thanking you in anticipation.

ACKNOWLEDGEMENTS

To the wonderful blogging and writing community to whom I owe so much. A big thank you to Colleen Chesebro for encouraging me to write poetry with her weekly poetry challenges. Also, I'd like to extend a thank you to Charli Mills at Carrot Ranch Literary Community for introducing me to flash fiction and for the opportunity to take part at zoom sessions reading our work at 5 at the mic. https://colleenchesebro.com/

https://carrotranch.com/

I'd like to mention the lovely little schemes like the local village community libraries.

Thank you to Sarah Northwood, for the digital image head shot of me.
https://www.sarahnorthwood-author.com/

ABOUT M J MALLON

 M J Mallon was born in Lion city Singapore, a passionate Scorpio with the Chinese Zodiac sign of a lucky rabbit. She spent her early childhood in Hong Kong. During her teen years, she returned to her father's childhood home, Edinburgh where she spent many happy years, entertained and enthralled by her parents' vivid stories of living and working abroad. Perhaps it was during these formative years that her love of storytelling began bolstered by these vivid raconteurs. She counts herself lucky to have travelled to many far-flung destinations and this early wanderlust has fuelled her present desire to emigrate abroad. Until that wondrous moment, it's rumoured that she lives somewhere in the UK, with her six-foot hunk of a rock god husband. Her two enchanting daughters have flown the nest but often return with a cheery smile.

Her motto is to always do what you love, stay true to your heart's desires, and inspire others to do so too, even it if appears that the odds are stacked against you like black hearted shadows.

MJ's favourite genres to write are YA fantasy, paranormal, ghost and horror stories, and various forms of poetry and flash fiction, because life should be sprinkled with a liberal dash of extraordinarily imaginative magic!

She celebrates bookish wonders, the spiritual realm and all things magical, mystical and mysterious at her blog home:
https://mjmallon.com/

ALSO BY M J MALLON

Next Chapter Publishing

YA Fantasy series, The Curse of Time

For details of publications please visit:

https://www.nextchapter.pub/authors/mj-mallon

Kyrosmagica Publishing

Poetry, Photography and Flash Fiction: *Do What You Love Fragility of your Flame*

https://books2read.com/u/mqXJq8

Poetry and Flash Fiction: *The Hedge Witch And The Musical Poet*

https://books2read.com/u/mv1OeV

Poetry, Prose and Photography: *Mr. Sagittarius*

http://mybook.to/MrSagittarius

An anthology: *This Is Lockdown*

Kindle: mybook.to/Thisislockdown

Paperback: mybook.to/Thisislockdownpb

Short Stories in Anthologies:

Bestselling horror compilations

Nightmareland compiled by Dan Alatorre

"Scrabble Boy" (Short Story)

Spellbound compiled by Dan Alatorre

"The Twisted Sisters" (Short Story)

Wings & Fire compiled by Dan Alatorre

"The Great Pottoo" (Short Story)

Ghostly Rites 2019 compiled by Claire Plaisted

"Dexter's Creepy Caverns" (Short Story)

Ghostly Rites 2020 compiled by Claire Plaisted

"No. 1 Coven Lane"

For all my publications and contributions to anthologies please refer to my author blog: https://mjmallon.com/

Amazon author page: https://www.amazon.co.uk/M-J-Mallon/e/B074CGNK4L/

SOCIAL MEDIA LINKS

Blog: https://mjmallon.com

Twitter: @Marjorie_Mallon

Amazon Author Page: https://www.amazon.co.uk/M-J-Mallon/e/B074CGNK4L/

Goodreads: https://www.goodreads.com/author/show/17064826.M_J_Mallon

Facebook: https://www.facebook.com/mjmallonauthor/

Instagram: https://www.instagram.com/mjmallonauthor/

Bookstagram: https://www.instagram.com/mjm_reviews/

Tiktok: https://www.tiktok.com@mjmallonauthor/

Bookbub: https://www.bookbub.com/authors/m-j-mallon

Authors, Bloggers Rainbow Support Club #ABRSC: https://www.facebook.com/groups/1829166787333493/

www.ingramcontent.com/pod-product-compliance
Lightning Source LLC
Chambersburg PA
CBHW020610130626
46552CB00007B/3138